When I Went to the Library

When I Went to the Library

EDITED BY

Debora Pearson

A GROUNDWOOD BOOK
DOUGLAS & McINTYRE
TORONTO VANCOUVER BUFFALO

Groundwood Books / Douglas & McIntyre
720 Bathurst Street, Suite 500, Toronto, Ontario M5S 2R4

Distributed in the USA by Publishers Group West
1700 Fourth Street, Berkeley, CA 94710

ONTARIO ARTS COUNCIL
CONSEIL DES ARTS DE L'ONTARIO

We acknowledge the financial support of the Canada Council for the Arts, the Ontario Arts Council and the Government of Canada through the Book Publishing Industry Development Program for our publishing activities.

National Library of Canada Cataloguing in Publication Data
Main entry under title: When I went to the library
ISBN 0-88899-423-0 (bound).–ISBN (0-88899-513-X (pbk.)
1. Children's stories, Canadian (English) I. Pearson, Debora
PS8321.W43 2001   jC813'.0108357   C2001-930784-5
Pz5.W518 2001

Library of Congress Control Number:: 2002106839

Designed by Michael Solomon
Cover illustration by Eric Beddows
Printed and bound in Canada by Friesens

CONTENTS

For children's librarians everywhere,
with affection and appreciation
DP

Editor's Note

THE public library—and the children's department in particular—has always been an important part of my life. When I was a little girl, I loved to go to the library and listen to the librarian read books out loud. Hearing her tell stories gave me the idea that I'd like to share books, words, and ideas with others too, when I grew up. Much later, warmed by those early memories, I went on to become a children's librarian and work in several branches of the Toronto Public Library. My favorite part of the job? Introducing books to young children and their parents.

Although I had left the library to work as an editor and writer of children's books, I never forgot my happy, formative times as a children's librarian. As the years passed, I realized that I wanted to do something to celebrate the rich history and traditions that I knew about and that had influenced me. Somehow, I wanted to give something back to the library.

I shared my thoughts with Patsy Aldana at Groundwood Books and proposed that I compile and edit an anthology of stories about books, reading, and the library. To my delight, Patsy gave the go-ahead. Along the way, she asked hard questions and helped me define and focus my ideas, ultimately turning the anthology into a better one than I had first envisioned. This book is the result.

My thanks and appreciation go out to the people at Groundwood: as well as Patsy, they include Lucy Fraser and Michael Solomon. I valued Lucy's editorial expertise, quiet efficiency, and thoughtful, approachable manner—she was both my sounding board and a frequently-consulted source of answers to my questions. I've often admired Michael's work as Groundwood's book designer and so it was a pleasure to know that his creative vision would help shape the book. He has made the anthology a lovely book to look at and an inviting one to read.

Many thanks, as well, to Eric Beddows for his wonderful cover illustration, and Michele Landsberg for her passionate, heartfelt introduction which so articulately sums up for me the importance of libraries for children. And most of all, I am grateful to the writers—Sarah Ellis, Jean Little, Celia Barker Lottridge, Ken Roberts, Ken Setterington, Marc Talbert, Budge Wilson, Tim Wynne-Jones, and Paul Yee—who each contributed an original selection to this anthology. Their stories about libraries, books, and reading are published here for the first time.

The worlds these writers have created—sometimes disquieting, sometimes lighthearted—are a reminder of their remarkable and diverse talents. It has been a privilege for me to work with each of them and witness their achievements up close.

Debora Pearson

When I Went to the Library: An Introduction

Michele Landsberg

I ALWAYS used to skip the introductions in books, just in case they let something slip and ruined the freshness of discovery that lay waiting for me in the pages ahead—or, worse, in case their dull, stodgy flavor slopped over and spoiled the distinctive tang of the story I was about to plunge into. Stories were so precious and exciting to me that I fiercely wanted to guard them from the ordinariness of daily life.

So I won't mind if you skip past this introduction and come back to it after you've enjoyed the stories. That was one good thing about introductions: they gave me a last, lingering, parting-is-such-sweet-sorrow taste of something I was sad to finish, the way you might munch on an apple core or the white of a watermelon rind after the juiciest part of the fruit is eaten.

∞

Back so soon? Then you already know that this book is about a fantastic place just a few blocks away from you—a palace that was built for you, whoever you are, and whose doors swing open freely to welcome you in. The library is like nothing else in our lives. It is free, it is voluntary—no one can make you go there—and all its treasures and pleasures are there to inform, entertain, delight, or transport you, as you please. You don't need to buy a ticket and, once you're in, with a book in your hands and your eyes beaming onto the page, you can travel through space and time and come back utterly transformed.

We didn't always have libraries, and they weren't always free. When they were first created, most ordinary families couldn't afford to buy books of their own. Going to the movies was a rare and expensive treat, television and computers didn't exist, and the Internet hadn't been dreamed of. So it was an amazing expression of concern for children, and for the public good, when governments and wealthy patrons helped to create "free stores" of books. Then a new profession was invented: children's librarian. These specialists are trained to know about books for young people and how to connect each reader with exactly the right story. The idea is pure happiness: no pressure, no nagging, no homework. The children's librarian has the selfless job of helping each young library user find what he or she is looking for, maybe without even knowing what that is.

When I went to the library for the first time, I felt as though I'd stepped into a fairy tale. The little door seemed to welcome me into a place as cozy as an enchanted cottage. Even the wood paneling of the entrance hall struck me as rich and strange. And I'd never imagined whole cliffs of books, rising rank on rank to the ceiling.

I was four years old, and my big brother—a U.S. Air Force pilot—had come home on furlough to discover that I could read, something that no one else in the family had noticed. He gave me the greatest gift of my life: he took me by the hand and walked me to the nearest children's library, St. Clements, to "sign me up." For the next eight years, the children's librarians—I remember two of them with love, Miss O'Brien and Miss St. John—treated me with kindness and respect. That was amazing. More than amazing—astounding. Everyone else in my life, however loving, had designs on me. My parents expected me to be a "good girl," a "little lady," and a model miniature woman with a taste for sewing, cooking, and pretty clothes. My teachers were intent on lockstep marching thirty of us at a time through a set curriculum of stuff to be memorized and spewed back on tests. No talking in class, no reading at recess, and please, no individuality. My piano teacher wanted me to be dutiful, to practice, and to pass music exams.

Only the children's librarians seemed genuinely happy to let me be. To let me be me. Tactfully, they would point out titles I might enjoy and then they would walk quietly away, so that I might not feel the slightest pressure to conform to their tastes. In the library, in books, I discovered a wild freedom— not just to learn for myself what gave me pleasure, but to live other lives, see through other eyes, go adventuring, sail, fly, suffer, defy, overcome, exult.

Nowhere else in my life could I taste such independence and such privacy. Reading, of course, is the most private act, as private as thinking or dreaming, but richer—because you're not alone in the book. You are silently in league with the author.

E. Nesbit and Arthur Ransome were my two most passionate favorites and, when I delighted in what they wrote, I felt as though they were including me—as an equal, a colleague, a secret sharer—

in the worlds they created. I was a lonely kid, because I didn't know any other readers or imaginers, but it didn't matter: in books, I was never lonely.

It was because of my lovely children's librarians that I was able to discover so many soul mates hiding behind the green covers of the thousands of books in the library. Fairy godmothers could not have been more powerful in my life. Because these librarians gave me the keys to the queendom of the mind, I grew up to become a writer. (There are no writers who don't start out as readers.)

You'll notice, in this book, that some librarians apparently act like ogres. The only ogre-ish librarians I ever met as a child (or, come to think of it, as a grown-up) were definitely, absolutely not children's librarians. I remember the darkly glowering adult librarian at St. Clements who fought as grimly as a pit bull to prevent me from using the adult library when I was twelve, when my children's librarians thought I was ready to move on up. (They were still looking out for me, trying to help me be me.) Like teachers, parents, or anyone else you meet, there can be disagreeable librarians—the "Shhh!" kind familiar from cartoons—but most who choose to train and work as children's librarians are the kind I remember. They want to help you discover the inner worlds within worlds: the intensity, mystery, excitement, and joy that lie between the covers of books.

This collection of short stories was dreamed up a few years ago to honor and celebrate the children's librarians who have been so instrumental in so many authors' lives. An anthology is something like a bag of licorice all-sorts: some stories have an outer coating of sweet sprinkles with a tart interior; some are layered, with each layer tasting slightly different. Some are like spirals, leading you into a surprising center. One story in this collection is about a writer trying to dispose of a dead librarian's ashes. Another concerns a mysterious vanishing boy who haunts the library—and has a weird sense of humor. Yet another story features a paper family that flies by night, powered by words.

Sad, funny, or strange, these stories are to be relished for themselves. Enjoy them. And remember that your children's librarian could be the truest friend of your life.

Dear Mr. Winston

Ken Roberts

DEAR Mr. Winston,

My parents said that I have to write and apologize. Dad says he is going to read this letter before it's sent and that I'd better make sure my apology sounds truly genuine. So, I am truly, genuinely sorry for bringing that snake into the library yesterday.

My parents say that what I did was wrong, even though the cardboard box was shut, most of the time, and there was no way that snake could have escaped if you hadn't opened the box and dropped it on the floor.

My parents say it's my fault for having brought that snake into the library and I truly, genuinely apologize but I still don't know how I was supposed to find out what kind of snake I had inside that box without bringing the snake right into the library so

I could look at snake pictures and then look at the snake and try to find a picture that matched the snake.

I told my parents something that I didn't get a chance to remind you about before the ambulance took you away. I did come into the library without the snake, first. I left the box outside, hidden under a bush and tried to borrow a thick green book with lots of snake pictures. You told me that the big green book was a reference book which meant that it had to stay inside the library and I couldn't take it out, even for ten minutes.

My parents say I still shouldn't have brought that snake into the library and that I have to be truly, genuinely sorry if I ever hope to watch *Galactic Patrol* on television again. My parents picked *Galactic Patrol* because it's my favorite show, although I'm not sure what not watching a television program has to do with bringing a snake into the library.

The people at the library say you hate snakes so much that you won't even touch a book with a picture of snakes on the cover and that is why you won't be back at the library for a few more weeks. If you want, you could watch *Galactic Patrol*. It's on at 4:00 P.M. weekdays, on channel 7. There are no snakes on the show because it takes place in space.

Did the flowers arrive? Dad picked them out but I have to pay for them with my allowance for the next two months. The flowers are proof that I am truly, genuinely sorry for having brought that snake into the library. I hope the people who work at the library find that snake soon! Did they look under all the chairs?

That snake isn't dangerous. It is a local snake, and there are no poisonous snakes in Manitoba. The people at the library say you know that too because that was one of the reasons you decided to move here. I bought that snake from a friend. I paid one month's allowance for it, which means that snake has cost me a total of three month's allowance and I only owned it for one hour!

Mom says I don't have to tell who sold me that snake so I won't tell you either because Dad says he is going to read this letter. Besides, I don't want you to be mad at anyone else when I am the one who brought that snake into the library yesterday. I am truly, genuinely sorry.

I want you to know that I didn't plan to show you that snake. I didn't mean to scare you at all. I knew where the big green snake book was kept. I put the box on a table close to the book and tried to find the right picture. I looked at a picture, then at the snake, at another picture, and then the snake. I did that five times and can tell you that the snake inside the library is not a python, a rattlesnake, an anaconda, an asp, or a cobra.

Anyway, I was surprised when you wanted to see what was inside the box because I didn't ask for any help and there were plenty of people in the library who did need help.

Dad says that the fact that I said, "Nothing," instead of "A snake," is proof that I knew I was doing something wrong when I brought that snake into the library. I am truly, genuinely sorry even though my friend Jake Lambert promised me that the snake I bought from him is perfectly harmless.

I did tell you that I didn't need any help and I did have a snake book open in front of me, so I don't know why you insisted on looking inside the box if you are so afraid of snakes and everything. I don't know why you picked up that box before opening a flap, either. If you had left the box on the table and maybe even sat down next to it, then maybe the box would have been all right when you screamed and fainted. You wouldn't have fallen so far, either, if you were sitting down.

Did you know that you broke out in a rash after

you fainted? I thought a person had to touch something like poison ivy to get a rash. I didn't know it was possible to get a rash by just thinking about something but my parents say it really can happen. I think maybe you did touch something. Maybe, when you were lying on the floor, that snake slithered over to you and touched you! Did you know that snake skin feels dry, not wet and slimy at all?

I just thought of something. Maybe everyone's looking in the library for that snake but it's not in the library. Maybe it crawled into one of your pockets or up your sleeve and rode with you to the hospital! Wouldn't that be funny? Why don't you get one of the nurses to check? If it's not in your clothes, it might have crawled out and might be hiding inside the hospital someplace. I think people should be looking there, too.

I am sure you will be talking to the people in the library, to make sure they find that snake before you go back to work. I hope they do find it, even though my parents say that I can't keep it. If that snake is found, could you ask the people at the library to give me a call? I would be interested in knowing that it is all right. And if they do find that snake and do decide to give me a call, could you ask them if they could compare that snake with the snake pictures in that big green reference book before they call me? I would still like to know what kind of snake I owned for an hour.

I am truly, genuinely sorry.

Your friend,

Cara

The Fall and Rise of
the Cut-Out Family

Sarah Ellis

THE Cut-Out family was born on the day that Delia was home from school with a cold. In the morning Delia listened to two stories and drank ginger ale through a bendy straw. For lunch she had chicken noodle soup and toast soldiers. After lunch she had a nap and when she woke up, she felt like making something. She wasn't allowed glue or paint in bed so she took some flyers out of the recycling box and cut out a family, the Cut-Out family.

Mrs. was from the World O' Linens ad. Boy was from the Hardware Depot discount book. Girl was from a Golden Temple Chinese take-out menu. Mr. was from the Computers R Us catalogue. Their sizes didn't match and Mrs. had no feet. But it didn't matter. As soon as Delia lined them up on her bedspread, they were a real family.

The Cut-Outs went skiing on Knee Mountain. Mrs. broke her arm and needed a Scotch tape cast. Girl got mad at Boy and called him "a stupid doo-doo head," so Mr. and Mrs. sent her for a time-out under the pillow. Mr. dyed his hair felt-tip green. They all went for a ride on the cat and then they told riddles and then they went to bed in a box of Kleenex.

Delia played with the Cut-Outs until dinner. The next day her nose stopped running, and she went back to school and soccer and her violin lessons. The Cut-Outs were thrown into the toy box under the bed. For a while they talked about their adventures on the slopes and their daring cat ride. They told their riddles again and again. They insulted each other. But gradually their voices grew thin and faint until finally they lay silent, staring wide-eyed into the dusty darkness. The Cut-Outs had run out of stories and jokes and memories. The Cut-Outs had run out of words.

Then suddenly, one day, a roaring sound filled the air, a snarling whine like some savage creature. The bedspread was whipped off the bed and the toy box was wrenched from under it. There stood Delia's mother, a spring-cleaning warrior armed with a duster, a mop and pail, a roaring vacuum cleaner, and a big plastic garbage bag. The Cut-Outs tumbled onto the bed as the toy box was over-turned. Girl hovered just above the garbage bag in Delia's mother's hand and then there was a pause. Delia's mother turned off the vacuum and sat down on the bed. She sorted through the lego and crayons and play-dough until she found the other members of the Cut-Out family. She smoothed out their bent bits and then set them up on the windowsill. There they stood, leaning against the cool glass, while Delia's mother dusted and sorted and vacuumed and sprayed and polished and left the room shiny and neat and silent.

Just as the door was closing, the sun came out from behind a cloud and streamed through the window. That was when the Cut-Outs discovered their true nature. They discovered they were made of words. Words were in every fiber of their being. Words showed faintly through them in the sunlight. Boy looked at Mrs. and read the message showing through her cotton velour housecoat. "Triple-layer cushions," he said.

"Me?" said Mrs. Immediately she felt a little taller, a little more substantial, a little more... three-dimensional.

"Read me," demanded Boy.

"All-purpose lubricant frees frozen nuts and bolts," said Girl. Boy felt power surging through him. "My turn," said Girl.

Mr. read her. "Chicken gai-ding with five precious vegetables."

Girl hugged the words to her. "Precious. Now you, Father." She peered through his snowy shirt. "It says, 'Bring in this flyer for further discounts.'"

"Flyer?" said Father. "Does that mean...?" He lifted slowly off the windowsill as though in a breeze. But there was no breeze. He hovered in mid-air. "Come on, everyone!" he cried. "We're flyers."

And the Cut-Outs were suddenly lighter than air. They floated up and around the room, tumbling and gliding, rolling and banking and looping the loop, talking and laughing. They spiraled up to the ceiling and out through an open skylight into the big world.

The Cut-Out family is still around. You might not have seen them because they lie low in the day. But at night they slip under doors and through letter-slots into libraries and bookstores. At night they read. For it is reading that keeps the Cut-Outs free and precious and triple-layered. It is reading that keeps the Cut-Outs alive.

Carlotta's Search

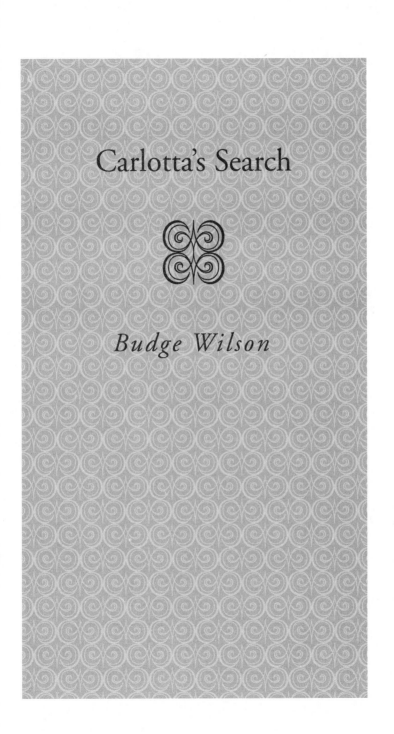

Budge Wilson

MOST people would have said that Carlotta Kirby's life seemed pretty normal. Her father was handsome and kind, and worked as a postal clerk in the Gladstone Postal Outlet. She had a brother, called Brett, who was really old—sixteen, in fact. She thought he was wonderful, and every time he'd bring home one of his football friends, she'd plan to marry him. If Brett brought two different friends in one week, it was tricky trying to decide which husband she'd prefer. But on the whole, Brett was pretty useless to her. He was always off doing his own thing and, when he was home, he often called her "Squirt." She could tell he thought she didn't matter. If you're sixteen years old, someone who's nine is worse than nothing.

Carlotta also had two uncles and three aunts, a

bedroom with mauve ruffled curtains, a six-speed bike, a best friend called Eleanor, and an orange cat named Marmalade. She had all those things. But if you asked her to tell you about her life, she'd just say, "My mom has leukemia."

The reason she knew her mother had leukemia was that she'd overheard her parents talking about it. "Today," said her mother in a whispery voice, "the doctor said I had to have chemotherapy for my leukemia." Carlotta was listening through the heat register and could hear everything—especially the way her mother started to cry with big heaving sobs. "My hair'll fall out," Mrs. Kirby croaked. She had beautiful thick black hair. Her father murmured some quiet, soothing things which Carlotta couldn't hear.

So Carlotta knew that much about the leukemia and the chemotherapy. But that's all she knew.

One day, when her father was in the yard raking the autumn leaves into a big pile, Carlotta went out and asked him what leukemia was. He looked at her hard. A nerve jumped in his cheek.

"Why are you asking about leukemia?" he said.

"Mom's got it," Carlotta said.

"How did you find out?"

"I heard," said Carlotta.

Her father gave her a big hug, a longer one than usual. "Don't worry about it," he said. "I'm sure it's going to be all right." There was something about that hug that worried Carlotta. And he hadn't told her a single thing.

She decided to ask her mother what leukemia was. Her mother was lying down on the living room sofa, when she should have been out in the kitchen getting dinner ready. It was five o'clock.

"What's leukemia?" asked Carlotta, without even saying "Hi," first.

Her mother looked very startled. "How...?" she said. "When...?"

"I heard," said Carlotta. "Last Tuesday."

Her mother shut her eyes for a moment. Finally she said, "It's a sickness, Carlotta. Lots of people have it. It's no big deal. They'll give me some stuff to make me better."

"Which'll make your hair fall out. *All* of it?"

Mrs. Kirby paused before answering. "Yes," she said. "I think so."

"You'll be *bald*?" Carlotta's eyes were wide, and bluer than usual.

"Yes." A tear squeezed out of Mrs. Kirby's left eye and dribbled down her cheek. "But I'll wear a big bandana. You won't see my head. You won't even notice. I often wear bandanas." Then she closed her eyes again. "I need to rest now," she said.

Carlotta stomped upstairs. She knew she ought to say something nice to her mother, or maybe kiss her. But she didn't. She was mad.

She went in her room. She didn't exactly slam the door, but she shut it with a pretty firm "thwack." She still didn't know anything worth knowing, and there was a hard knot of anger in her chest. Marmalade was lying on her bed, so she picked him up and hugged him. But even that didn't make her feel better.

Why was her mother sick? She'd kept telling them all to get lots of exercise. She also handed out vitamins, and served lots of milk and whole wheat bread and fruit, so that the whole family would stay healthy. But did her mom do all those things and eat all that stuff? Carlotta had never noticed if she did or she didn't. She certainly wasn't healthy, so it must be all her own fault. How could she not practise what she preached? It wasn't fair. There was an apple on Carlotta's bureau and she picked it up and threw it into the wastebasket. Then she dug a big soggy chocolate bar out of her desk drawer. Her mother wasn't the only one who could break the rules. And since her mother was obviously not

going to cook any dinner that night, she'd better eat
something.

Later, they had pizza for supper. A boy came and
delivered it at half past six. Carlotta hated pizza.

At eight o'clock, Carlotta went upstairs and
knocked on Brett's door. He was listening to some
loud music which Carlotta pretended to like, but
didn't. "Come in!" he shouted.

"What's leukemia?" she yelled. She yelled so loud
that he heard it above the electric guitars and crash-
ing cymbals and drums. He turned off his sound
system.

"C'mere," he said. He was sitting on the floor.
She went and sat beside him. This made her very
nervous. He'd never asked her to sit beside him
before. Never. "Look, Squirt," he said, and put his
arm around her shoulder. This made her even more
uneasy. "It's OK. It's gonna be just fine. You're too
young to worry about junk like that." He gave her
a friendly little punch on the same shoulder. "Go to
bed," he said. "Get your beauty sleep."

Junk! What she wanted to know was certainly
not *junk*!

Later, Carlotta's dad came up and kissed her good
night and tucked her in. That's what Mom always
used to do.

"Where's Mom?" asked Carlotta.

"She went to bed early," he said. "She's not feeling too perky tonight." Then he added, "You can't expect parents to be strong and cheerful *all* the time, you know."

Why not? thought Carlotta. *That's what parents are for.* She turned over and pretended she'd fallen asleep. She even concocted a gentle, deep little snore.

The next day in school, Carlotta met Eleanor at the swing set during recess.

"What's leukemia?" said Carlotta.

"Why?" said Eleanor. "Who's got it?"

"Mom," said Carlotta.

"Oh," said Eleanor. There was a long silence.

"Well?" urged Carlotta.

Eleanor sighed. "It's a kind of sickness, I guess. Maybe like a cold or the flu or something. I dunno. Ask your dad."

It was Carlotta's turn to sigh. "I did," she said. Her throat was suddenly tight, and she was afraid she might cry or yell or throw something at somebody. She ran back to the school entrance and went in. *I'll hide in the classroom,* she thought, *until recess is over.* She felt like she was going to burst wide open, and she didn't want to do it in front of the whole school.

But her teacher, Miss Cassidy, was in her class-room. Carlotta didn't see her at first, because she was down on her hands and knees behind the desk, pick-ing up about five million paper clips she'd dropped. Miss Cassidy was young, with red flyaway hair and a big smile. She wasn't a very serious-looking teacher. By the time she stood up, Carlotta was at her seat, with her face down on the desk, hidden by her arms.

"Carlotta!" Miss Cassidy's voice was worried and kind. "What's wrong?"

Carlotta jumped a bit on her chair. She'd thought she was alone. "Nothing," she said.

Then Miss Cassidy put her hand on her shoulder, very softly. "Tell me," she said.

That did it. Suddenly Carlotta started to cry. She cried hard and out loud, just like the kid next door who was only three years old. She went through the four Kleenexes that Miss Cassidy put in her hand. She felt like she'd never stop crying. But finally she did. About one minute before the bell rang, she was able to speak.

"My mom's got leukemia. No one will tell me what it is. She's tired all the time. Her hair is going to fall out. I'm mad at everybody. I'm even mad at *her*. *Why won't anyone tell me anything?*"

Miss Cassidy only had time to say one thing

before the bell rang and the kids started to pour back into the classroom. "Meet me in the library this afternoon after school's over," she said.

&&

When Carlotta went up to the school library at 3:15 that afternoon, Miss Cassidy was already sitting at a table with five books piled up beside her. She was running her fingers through her wild hair and taking notes. There were volumes from three encyclopedias, one novel about a young girl with leukemia, and a medical reference book.

"OK, Carlotta," she said. "Both of us will start searching. I don't know too much about leukemia either, so we can both hunt for answers." She showed Carlotta how to look up the right pages by checking indexes and tables of contents. She said, "You start with that book, and I'll start with this one. We'll share what we find out."

A while later, Carlotta said, "Leukemia is a kind of cancer. That's bad. It's not just the flu."

"No, it's not. And yes, it's not good. But I've also just read that some forms of leukemia can be treated very successfully. In this book, it mentions a man who had chemotherapy for his leukemia twenty years ago, and is still healthy and working at his job."

They read for another half hour or so in silence. Then Carlotta spoke. "This chemotherapy thing sounds really cool," she said. "But it makes your hair fall out."

"But it grows back," said Miss Cassidy. "And I just learned that it sometimes comes back curly!"

"But you throw up."

"Sometimes, yes. But they have a wonderful new drug that often prevents that."

"Who told you that?" Carlotta was doubtful.

"This medical book. Here, have a look yourself." Miss Cassidy shoved it across the table.

Carlotta flipped through the pages. She was a fast reader, and could often get the sense of things by just skimming her eyes across the lines of print. She'd already discovered that it wasn't her mother's *fault* that she was sick. But there were other things to worry her.

"Sometimes people die," Carlotta said. She'd learned about that in the very first book she'd opened. Now she felt she was ready to talk about it— *needed* to talk about it. Terrible though the fact was, she had to say it out loud. She had to feel that the fact was out there in the air, instead of squashed inside her head.

"Yes," said Miss Cassidy. "And sometimes they don't."

It felt good to get *that* thought out into the space between Miss Cassidy and herself. Suddenly Carlotta stood up. "It's four thirty," she said. "I have to be home by five, or Mom gets worried I've been kidnapped or something. Maybe I'll take the novel with me."

Miss Cassidy picked up the other four books and said, "Watch me while I put them back on the shelves. Then you'll know where to find them when you need them."

"Thanks a bunch, Miss Cassidy," said Carlotta, as she put on her jacket. Then she added, "Sorry to use up your Kleenex. But it sure felt good to do all that howling."

"I like to have a little cry, myself, from time to time," said Miss Cassidy. "It sort of loosens the kinks. Perhaps you could let your mom do some of that howling."

"Yeah. I s'pose you're right. And try to get fond of pizza. That's what Dad keeps bringing home when Mom's too tired to cook. Or I could maybe learn to make something I like. If Mom has a good day tomorrow, I'll ask her to give me a lesson in scrambling eggs. I like eggs. What else? Not broccoli. Unless someone says it's a cure for leukemia. Maybe peas. Peas are OK. Or even something spectacular like chocolate pudding."

Miss Cassidy pointed to a shelf in the library. "There are three or four cookbooks over there," she said, "written especially for kids."

"Some place!" said Carlotta as she walked with Miss Cassidy towards the door.

"Right!" laughed Miss Cassidy. Her crazy red hair jiggled up and down. "Some place!"

◉◉

As Carlotta walked home, it started to get a little bit dark. The sky was a sort of purple color behind the rooftops, and the bare trees were silhouetted against the sky. She could see how beautiful that was, but she was glad when the streetlights suddenly came on, bringing out the late green of the lawns and the colored wooden houses. She could hear the banging and thudding of boxes and machinery down by Halifax harbor, and she listened to the deep-throated horn of a ship as it moved into sheltered water. She liked those sounds. She hadn't noticed or heard these things, for a long time. She'd been shut up inside herself, with her own thoughts and fears keeping everything else out.

Carlotta realized that, in some ways, nothing had changed. Her mother was still very ill, and nobody at home wanted to talk about it. But even if they didn't, she knew exactly where she could go for help—for a lot of things, not just about leukemia. She wasn't sure how to describe what she was feeling, but the word that jumped into her mind was: *free*. It was as though some sort of door had opened, and she was able to go through it. On this particular day, that was enough for Carlotta.

Anna Marie's Library Book and What Happened to It

Celia Barker Lottridge

There once was a girl called Anna Marie
Who borrowed a book from the library,
   It was a fat book,
   It was a blue book,
   And its title promised:
   Everything about Dogs
   Stories and poems
   And pictures and facts:
   EVERYTHING about dogs!

Anna Marie came home with her book,
She sat down in the kitchen and started to look;
   She loved dogs,
   She loved stories and poems and pictures
   And facts.
   She even loved blue!
   She loved EVERYTHING about this book.

Her brother Ted came home from school,
He looked over her shoulder and he said, "Cool,
    I'm doing a report on golden retrievers;
    I need facts,
    I need pictures,
    And a story would be good.
    Can I borrow the book? Please?"

"Well, all right," said Anna Marie. "Just till
    tomorrow."

But the next day...

Ted's best friend Joe came over to play,
He saw the book and he said, "Hey,
    I need a poem about an animal;
    A dog is an animal,
    And right here's a poem!
    Can I borrow the book? Please?"

"Well, all right," said Ted. "Just till tomorrow."

But the next day...

Ms. Cubbin, Joe's teacher, said to the class,
"That poem's so good that I think I'll ask
    Joe to lend me that book.
    I might find more treasures and share them with
      you.
    Could I borrow it? Please?"

"Well, all right," said Joe. "Just till tomorrow."

But the next day...

Ms. Cubbin's small girl on the drive to her sitter,
Opened the book, fell in love with one picture,
    "Dog!" she said. "Dog!"
    She would not turn the page
    Nor let go of the book.
    She lugged it into the house.
    The sitter said, "Well, I hope we can borrow it."

"I suppose it's all right," said Ms. Cubbin. "Just till
    tomorrow."

But the next day...

The sitter's tall son, while he munched on his toast,
Said, "Ma, this is the story I've always loved most;
   It's about an adventurous dog who runs away
   And gets into trouble and then he comes home,
   I want to read it again.
   Could I borrow the book? Please?"

"Well, all right," said his mother. "Just till
   tomorrow."

That very same day...

Anna Marie took a long long bus ride
To her music lesson and there by her side,
   Sat a high school student reading a book;
   A fat book,
   A blue book,
   A book about dogs.

"I have to ask," said Anna Marie,
"Did you get that book from the library?"
   The boy was just a little surprised;
   "No," he said, "My ma loaned it to me.
   No problem with that, is there?"

"But I'm quite sure," said Anna Marie,
"That fat blue book was borrowed by me,
Straight from the shelves of the library.
Look at page 30 and you will see
The shoelace I used for a bookmark.
    But I loaned the book to my brother Ted,
    Now somehow you have it!
    This is completely confusing.
    Maybe your ma could return it to…someone,
    And somehow it will get back to me.
    You see—I want to read it!"

So the boy returned the book
To his ma
Who gave it, not to the baby, of course,
But straight to her mother, Ms. C.
Who returned it to Joe
Who returned it to Ted
Who returned it to Anna Marie.
    He said, "I don't know what happened—
    Has it really been a week?"

"Something strange happened," said Anna Marie,
"So after this USE THE LIBRARY!"

And she read the book from cover to cover,
Then she returned it...
And took out another.

Mrs. Grinny Pig, Tiggle Wiggle, and Henry

Jean Little

HENRY Higham did his best to keep clear of the school Media Resource Center. That was the new name for the library now that it had a row of computers and the video stuff. But it wasn't the library itself Henry really minded; it was Mrs. Grinstag, the librarian who had taken Mrs. Moyer's place while she was on maternity leave. Mrs. Grinstag came to Sunnyfield School on a dark day in January and, for Henry, she made it darker still.

"Grinny Pig is a royal pain," he grumbled to his best friend, Doug.

"My sister likes her a lot," Doug said mildly. Doug was a much calmer boy than Henry. "She's going to join the Book Lovers' Club. She wouldn't be one of Mrs. Moyer's Library Friends because they worked all the time shelving books and putting cards in them. Grinny Pig promised they'd read poetry and discuss books. She even said they might have a Book Lovers' sleep over one night during March break."

"Girls!" jeered Henry. "G.P. is a pain in the butt and you know it."

"If I were you, I guess I'd agree," Doug said, shooting Henry a sympathetic glance. "But you're the one who started everybody calling her 'Grinny Pig.' Aren't you doing the same thing?"

Henry grinned. He thought it was the best teacher's nickname he had ever heard. All the kids, even the girls who followed her around like Mary's lamb, called Mrs. Grinstag "Grinny Pig" behind her back. But that was the difference. She never heard her nickname; everybody heard his.

"Doug," he growled, "if anyone gets smart and calls me 'Huggie,' I'll kill him."

"Not bad," Doug said, snickering. "Maybe I should tell Edward—"

Henry turned on his friend with such a ferocious look that Doug backed up and raised his hands in surrender.

"OK, OK. I won't. I tried to make her stop, remember?"

Henry did. At their first library period, Mrs.

Grinstag had beamed at him and said, "Henry! That's perfect. You look exactly the way I imagine Henry Huggins looking. And your surname even begins with an *H*."

Doug spoke quickly. "It's 'High-am.' You don't say the *g* in it. It's not like 'Huggins' really."

"I know, I know," she said. Her big smiling teeth looked like piano keys. "But Henry Huggins is a great boy, so I'm paying Henry Higham a compliment."

Doug was stumped. But Henry knew it had been too late from the moment she mentioned the name "Huggins." He sat and stared out the window and wished she would drop dead. She didn't, and the damage was done. That Friday, after Henry got four baskets in a game, even the coach said, "Well done, Huggins!"

Even before Grinny Pig took over, Henry had not been overly fond of Mrs. Moyer's library. It was designed to help kids do projects. Henry Higham hated working on projects. He had no interest in the lives of insects, how to build skyscrapers, what life in a submarine was like, or how ancient Egyptians mummified people. He liked reading comics where the picture did more than half the work. When he did read a whole book, it was usually one from his older brother's collection. Before Chris left for college, he had handed over a couple of big cartons full of *Hardy Boys* books and some by Eric Wilson, Martyn Godfrey, and Gordon Korman. Henry liked them because you knew exactly what to expect and there was lots of talking and adventure. The Korman ones made him laugh out loud. So Henry avoided the library. The trouble was that projects loomed ahead.

"You children are so lucky to have Mrs. Grinstag for your school librarian," his mother said one night. "She's helping collect things for the auction to raise money for your school. In one half hour last night, she did more sorting than all the rest of us put together. She is so organized. Henry, don't feed Frank at the table."

"Organized isn't all she is," Henry muttered as he let the Higham's fat cat eat the burned end of his fish stick. Frank was the only family member who had heard of Henry's problems with Grinny Pig. If Manda, his sister, ever heard that the librarian called him "Henry Huggins," he would never live it down. She'd blab to Chris the next time he came home and Henry would be called "Huggins" forever. Thank goodness Manda was in high school and never met up with the kids from Sunnyfield.

"She's coming over in a few minutes to pick up some things," Henry's mother went on. "If you want to reclaim anything before—"

Henry choked. His mother stopped talking while he wheezed.

"She's coming to this house?" he gasped, the moment he had breath enough to speak. "Grinny Pig is coming HERE?"

Mrs. Higham stared coldly at her younger son. "Mrs. Grinstag should be here any minute," she said.

"I'm out of here!" Henry yelped, jumping up so fast his chair overturned.

"Sit down, Henry," his father said. "Pick up the chair, reseat yourself, and ask to be excused. I won't have my children behaving like hooligans."

"Excuse me, please," Henry begged, his rear end hovering above the chair seat.

"You are excused," Dad said.

But the doorbell chimed before Henry could escape. His mother, coming after him to nag, opened the door and there, large as life, stood Grinny Pig herself.

Henry tried to slip past. Frank, faithful old Frank, trotted after him as usual. As Henry's foot hit the bottom step, Mrs. Grinstag's laughing voice sang out, "Ribsy! That animal must be Ribsy. Am I right, Henry Huggins?"

"Henry, say hello to Mrs. Grinstag," Mrs. Higham said in a tone of steel.

"Hi, Mrs. Grinny…stag," Henry mumbled, thoroughly rattled. "His name's Frank. Mom named him after Frank Sinatra. I got homework. Please excuse me."

He raced up the stairs but he could still hear their voices.

"I love teasing Henry," he heard old Grinny Pig telling Manda and his parents. "Doesn't he make you think of Henry Huggins?"

Manda drawled, "Not really. Henry reminds me of Ramona the Pest."

Nobody mentioned Grinny Pig at breakfast. Henry doubted their chivalry would last once Chris came home. But Chris did not come home until Easter and by then, even at school, Henry's hated nickname had been largely forgotten. Several other kids had been given Grinny Pig nicknames too. "Pippi," "Dickon," and "Minerva" were some of them. None were as bad as "Huggins."

Henry went on avoiding the Resource Center. He completed one project using his parents' books and the Internet. When another was assigned, he got the brilliant idea of doing his research in the public library. It was a long way from his house though and he still had three weeks before the project was due. No need to rush things.

"Henry, how would you like to spend twenty bucks?" Manda asked him that Friday evening.

"What's the catch?"

"You have to spend it at that auction to raise money for Sunnyfield. Mom's helping to run the dumb thing and she told me I'd have to come and spend twenty dollars. I want you to go instead. I have other plans."

Henry looked over her offer with care and, once he was sure there were no hidden strings, he took the money. He was excited about the idea of having to spend twenty bucks. Usually someone was at him to save, but not today. And who knew what might turn up? He made up his mind to practise bidding on things he was sure Manda's money wouldn't buy. That way, he'd have the fun of hoping a little before somebody outbid him. He tried to buy a computer with lots of CD-ROMs, a keyboard, a crokinole table in perfect condition, and a ticket to go on a cruise in the West Indies. He always got bid down but it was fun while it lasted.

Then the auctioneer held up a smallish aquarium.

"This exotic African pygmy hedgehog would cost at least one hundred dollars in any pet store," he said, smiling like the wolf in Little Red Riding Hood. "Come on, you yuppies. Here's just the pet for an apartment. A sweet little Mrs. Tiggle Wiggle all your own. Who'll give me fifty?"

"Twenty," said Henry, as a joke. He was wondering if he should explain to the guy later that the Beatrix Potter hedgehog was really named "Mrs. Tiggy-Winkle" when the auctioneer called out, "Sold! To the young man in the Blue Jays shirt."

Henry had on his Jays sweatshirt but he still could not believe that the hedgehog was his. He stood clutching Manda's twenty-dollar bill until a lady swept down on him, beaming, and plucked it out of his hand.

"Come and get it, dear," she said. "The pet shop lady who donated it left an envelope for you. It gives instructions on how to care for your new pet. I think it's sweet but it hisses and puts up its prickles whenever I go near."

In a daze, Henry listened while somebody told him that the donor wanted the aquarium returned. He was given some cat kibble and a tin of dried crickets.

"My nephew has one. It likes live food best," said

someone from the crowd watching him collect his purchase. The instructions told him to drop by the store for anything he needed, and that the hedgehog was a boy. Henry headed home with the hedgehog hissing and looking like an agitated pincushion.

His father bore up well under the shock. "You're lucky we have an aquarium in the basement," he said, "or you'd be paying for one with your allowance."

Frank bushed up his fur in a cat imitation of a hedgehog. Tiggle Wiggle hissed louder in response. Once the aquarium was set up and Henry had returned from the pet store with advice and supplies, he sat on his bed and stared glumly at what he had bought himself. Frank prowled around, looking murderous.

"Hey, maybe I can turn you into a project," Henry told the bundle of prickles as he sucked his sore fingers.

A week later, Henry had grown fond of Tig. He no longer was hissed at once the hedgehog had checked his scent. Henry had even managed to pick him up wearing only one protective glove.

Tig was nocturnal and scuffed and scurried around his aquarium all night; he also loved to go for walks outside his glass home. But he travelled fast and was good at vanishing. Once he found himself a dark corner, he would just lie there, savoring his freedom.

Henry's mother dug out the wicker cat carrier they had bought for Frank when he was small. It was just right for the tiny hedgehog and Henry used it to take Tig on excursions to the park or down by the river. The only problem with the basket was an insecure latch but Henry was careful to keep the lid tightly closed and Tig did not realize it was loose.

The deadline for Henry's project on animals was coming fast. Although Frank had, by this time, made his peace with Tig, Henry disliked leaving the two pets on their own. He had visions of Frank with a nose bristling with prickles. Putting Tig into the cat carrier, Henry set out for the public library.

"No *Hardy Boys* there, Henry," Manda said. "They don't stock trash."

There was no librarian behind the desk, just a young man reading a book. He seemed oblivious to the world around him.

"Where's the librarian?" asked Henry.

"Here," said the young man, laying aside his book with obvious reluctance. "How can I help you?"

"Do you have any *Hardy Boys*?" Henry asked, checking on Manda's story.

"No," said the young man. "You can get them other places. I'll bet you've already got enough to sink a ship."

Henry wondered how he knew. He scowled.

"I like them," he said, stung by the scorn he heard. "I like them better than whatever that is you're reading."

The young man glanced down at the book and smiled.

"I'll make you a small wager," he said. "You go over there and sit down and read the first five pages of this book, without skipping, and I'll bet you beg me to let you take it home and finish it."

"What'll I get if it bores me?" asked Henry.

"Two bucks," the guy said instantly. "I'm reading it for the third time."

Henry shoved the cat basket under the table, out of harm's way. Then he began to read *Maniac Magee* by Jerry Spinelli. He was on page 10 before he knew it. And he did not want to stop.

He stood up to go to the desk and saw, with a sinking heart, that the lid of the cat carrier was open and Tiggle Wiggle had vanished. Henry and the librarian hunted high and low. Other kids who dropped in joined in the search. Then the young man got a book on hedgehogs off the shelf.

"Read," he said to Henry. "Maybe it'll give us some pointers."

The book, to Henry's surprise, told exactly the sorts of places in which hedgehogs liked to hide. But as he started to tell the man, there was a shriek from the staff room and Mrs. Grinstag herself came hopping out, clutching a boot and screaming, "Harry, there's a hissing wild creature in my boot!"

The young man tried hard not to laugh as he tipped Tig out of the footwear and back into the basket. Henry clapped it shut.

"Thanks for the coffee and short respite. I must fly, I'm late already!" the school librarian said, yanking on her boot and heading for the door. "Get home on time for once, Harry."

Henry held on to the cat carrier with one hand and shoved the book across the desk with the other.

"I want it," he said. "It's great. Is it good all the way to the end?"

"Yes," the young man said. "I knew you would like it, Henry."

"How do you know my name?" Henry stopped then began again. "How do you know—?"

"How do I know Grinny Pig? Don't worry about

it, Henry Huggins. After all, she calls me 'The Dirty Dog,'" the young man said, laughing. Then he leaned forward and whispered, "Grinny Pig is my mother!"

Henry laughed all the way home.

He got an A plus on his project. Before he turned it in, he put an acknowledgment on page 2:

"This report would not have been written without the help of a Dirty Dog."

Rose's Wish

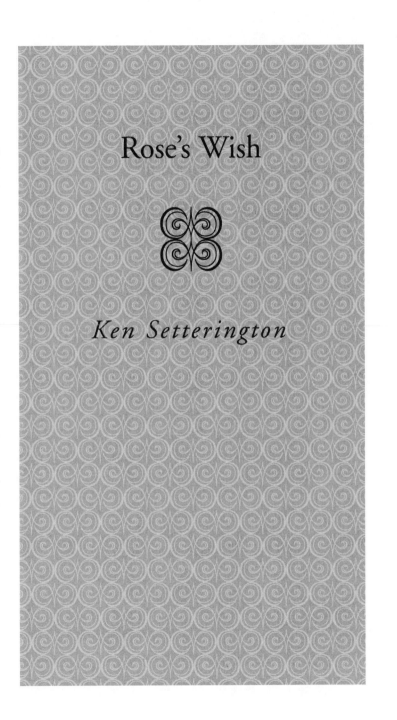

Ken Setterington

"I DIDN'T do it, honest."

"Honestly," the old woman corrected, "I didn't do it, honestly. Don't worry honey, I didn't say that you did."

She looked around the elevator, then back at the buttons. They were all lit up. Mark stood in the back corner eyeing the woman. He had seen her a few times since he had moved into the building, but he had never spoken to her before.

"So what wise butt do you think did this?" she asked, pointing to the buttons with a bouquet of daisies.

Mark shrugged his shoulders. He wished the doors would close so they could be on their long journey upwards. Finally, the doors shut. The two were off to the second floor. The doors opened, Mark pressed the "Close" button, and they went on to the third.

"Anyone can see I'm too old to walk up to the fourteenth floor. What's your excuse?"

Mark looked at the old woman again. She was a little bit short, a little bit chubby, and a little bit strange. Most adults hardly ever talked to other adults when they got on the elevator, and they never talked to kids. This woman was talking to him as though she actually thought what Mark had to say was important.

"I'd walk to the sixteenth floor," he said, "but there's always big kids hanging out on the sixth-floor stairs with this big dog that barks like crazy."

When they reached the seventh floor, she announced, "Safe from the big kids and the dog on the stairs."

"Safe," agreed Mark.

She held up her flowers. "Don't you just love daisies? People think they're plain, but to me each one of them is special." She reached into her bouquet and pulled out a flower. Then she slipped the daisy into his buttonhole.

Mark had never worn a flower and he wasn't sure that he wanted to, but he smiled and said, "Thanks."

"Oh here I am—the fourteenth floor." She started out of the elevator. "By the way, my name is Emms."

"I'm Mark. Bye…Emms."

Emms didn't look back to see Mark wave. She just walked down the long corridor and called back, "Bye, Mark."

Mark pulled out the daisy, smelled it, then put it in his pocket. He didn't want anyone to see him wearing a flower.

⟡

Mark was coming home from school the next time he saw Emms. She was carrying a large porcelain jar and standing by the steps leading to the apartment building doors.

"Hi Emms." Mark felt good having someone to say "Hi" to when he got home. They started up the stairs together and went into their building.

"That looks heavy," said Mark. "Can I carry it for you?"

"Oh no, dear. I kind of like carrying it." They got into the elevator. "But it is getting a little heavy."

"Why don't you put it down?"

"I wouldn't put my best friend on the dirty floor of an elevator. This jar contains the ashes of Rose Reader. She was my best friend."

Mark stared at the jar. Ashes! Of a *dead* person? Is that what Emms meant?

"Really, she died last week. I picked up her ashes

today, so I'm feeling kind of down. It is a pretty jar though, isn't it? I think Rose would have liked it."

"Who was Rose?" Mark glanced at the jar again.

"She was a librarian and she could tell wonderful stories." Emms traced the pattern on the jar with her finger. "I miss her."

"I'm sorry," said Mark.

"Thanks—oh, here I am, the fourteenth floor. You know, it's really the thirteenth floor but it's called the fourteenth because thirteen is bad luck. But I think I got lucky today. I met you again and I know that we are going to be friends now."

She got off the elevator. "Bye, Mark."

Mark smiled. He had no idea that those ashes would cement their friendship.

◌◌

When Mark saw Emms next, she was in the garden beside their building.

"Mark, come here and look at these peonies. They're so majestic and—oh look, a butterfly. Don't you just love butterflies?"

"Yes," mumbled Mark.

"What's bothering you?"

"Nothing."

"Tell me about nothing."

"I have speech arts on Friday and I don't have a

speech. I have to give a talk for ten minutes and I hate standing up in front of the class."

"Can you tell a story for this speech arts?"

"The teacher said that you could recite a poem."

"Then you can tell a story," Emms smiled. "And you, my friend, have come to the best person to teach you how to tell a story." She led him inside. "I'll help you find a story for speech arts."

Mark had never seen anything like Emms's apartment. Books were piled everywhere: on the floor, on the sofa, on the tables, and in the bookcases that covered the walls. Mark was looking in one bookcase when he noticed four copies of the same book. They were written by Winnifred E. Walsh. Five other books were also written by this person.

"I see you have discovered my books," Emms said. "I'll tell you about those some other time, but now we have to get a story for you." She pointed to the jar which was on an old, richly carved chair. "It's too bad that Rose can't help us. She always knew the best stories...

"Now I can't teach you everything about storytelling in just three days," she continued, "but I can make certain you can tell one story by Friday. What kinds of stories do you like? Funny ones, scary ones—"

"Scary!"

"Then I have a great one for you. It's an old English fairy tale, *Mr. Fox*, and it's guaranteed to make you shiver." She moved some books from an armchair for Mark and told him the story.

"Be bold, be bold, but not too bold, lest that your heart's blood should run cold…" Her voice was strong and clear. She didn't use crazy voices or wave her arms about. She just sat there, sharing the story with him. As she did, the room seemed to disappear and shivers ran up and down Mark's spine.

"That was great!" he shouted at the end. "But I could never do that."

"Sure you can," said Emms. "It just takes practice." She looked at him closely. "See the story in your mind, then tell your audience what you see. When you can see the story, then you can tell it."

She pulled a book from one of the bookcases and handed it to Mark. "The story is in here."

For three days, he mumbled the story to himself as he walked to and from school. At home, he told the story to the bathroom mirror over and over again and doodled pictures of the story. After school on Thursday, he told the story to Emms one last time.

"You're ready," she announced. "Tomorrow your

classmates will listen, then tell the story to others."

The next day after school, Mark rushed back to the apartment to tell Emms about speech arts. He was shocked to find her in the garden, sitting in a wheelchair with her leg in a cast.

"What happened to you?" he cried out.

"Oh, this is nothing. I slipped on the floor at the Y after my aqua-fit class and broke my ankle. I had to be taken to the hospital in a wet bathing suit. I am just glad to be home and in real clothes! Now tell me about your storytelling."

"It was amazing! I watched the story unfold in my mind and told the class what I saw. It felt as though they were all with me."

Emms smiled. "You have the gift, my friend. You are a storyteller."

Then she looked at Mark and, in a low voice, said, "I want to ask you a huge favor, but no one can know about it. I promised Rose that I would bury her ashes under the new library building. Will you go to where the old library stood and see if they have begun digging the foundation for the new building? If they have, we must move fast and figure out a way to get the ashes in there."

Mark looked at his watch. "I can go there right now."

ଚ୬

The old library was gone. In its place was a fence of tall boards. There were viewing holes cut into the wood but they were too high for Mark to look through. Mark walked slowly around the fence until he found a gap at the bottom of one of the boards. The gap looked just about big enough to fit him, so he got down on his hands and knees and started to squeeze through it. He was almost on the other side when he heard the dog. It was barking and it sounded big.

Mark froze, then shimmied back as fast as he could. The barking turned into growls as the dog reached the inside of the fence.

"What are you doing there, boy?" called a man from over the fence.

"Nothing," said Mark, standing up. He could still hear the dog growling. "I just wanted a closer look."

"Can't see much—just a big hole. They start building sometime next week. Run along now."

Mark did. He had to tell Emms about the problems that faced them: a high fence, a security guard, and a really mean dog.

ଚ୬

"Oh that's nothing," laughed Emms, after Mark

recounted what he had found. "We can deal with those things. Our real problem is Mrs. MacKiver."

"Who's that?"

"An old battle-ax who's been yelling at people for years. She's the head of the library. She does a good job, but she isn't very nice—no one likes her. Everything has to be done her way."

"Did Rose like her?"

"Heavens no! She and Rose were always arguing. Rose was a terrific children's librarian and everyone liked her. She was known everywhere. I think Connie MacKiver was jealous of Rose. Connie never cared for children, stories, or what people thought about the library. These days, she just wants lots of computers to get information faster."

Emms shook her head. "It's too bad—they could have been a terrific team, information and stories. But Rose and Connie argued from the first day they worked together. Actually, I think they were both a little foolish—it takes two to argue and neither of them wanted to stop."

She stopped for a moment and looked over at the peonies. "A few months ago, when Rose knew she was dying, she asked me to put her ashes in the foundation for the new library. Rose's wish is important to me. She deserves to be part of the library."

"What will we do about the fence, the guard, and the dog? And what about Mrs. MacKiver?"

"Come by tomorrow evening around six o'clock," replied Emms. "We'll take Rose's ashes to the site and see if we can figure out something."

That night, as Mark lay in bed, he worried about the ashes. Was it illegal to scatter them? Could they be arrested? What about the dog? He tried to calm himself by remembering his success as a storyteller, but he didn't sleep much that night.

Mark pushed Emms in her wheelchair out of their building and down the street to the site of the library. The jar was on her lap.

"It really was my lucky day when I met you," said Emms. "I only wish that you had known Rose. You would have liked her and I know that she would have liked you."

They slowed down when they reached the site. There was no sign of the guard or dog as Mark pushed Emms around the fence. When they were halfway around, Emms announced, "This is the spot. I can see right through that crack, right to the bottom of the hole."

She put on the brakes to her wheelchair and stood up, still holding the jar, to make room for

Mark. He climbed onto the seat, then onto the arms of the wheelchair. "I can see over the fence," he said, scanning the site. "I still don't see the dog."

Emms opened the jar and pulled out a large, plastic bag filled with ashes. She gently opened the bag and handed it to Mark. Mark gingerly took the bag. He had expected the ashes to look like cigarette ashes, but these looked more like a bag of crushed shells mixed with ash. He was holding ashes of bones.

"Winnifred E. Walsh, what do you think you are doing here?" The shrill voice startled them. A sharp-faced woman had come up behind them. "I knew you would try something."

Emms's voice was clear and strong. "Connie MacKiver, these are Rose's ashes and they are going to be at the bottom of the new library. That was her wish. My friend here and I are going to help her get her wish and so are you."

"Absolutely not," the other woman replied. "I always thought Rose was a little crazy, but now I think that *you* are completely nuts. Rose's ashes will not be part of this library. I don't want anyone thinking that it is a memorial to some batty children's librarian, no matter how great you say she was. Give that bag to me."

She reached up to grab the ashes from Mark who was still balanced on the arms of the chair. As she did, her fingernails dug into the bag, tearing a hole. Mark clutched the bag, twisted away from her, and fell into the chair.

Mrs. MacKiver lunged again for the bag. Mark looked for Emms, then tossed the bag to her. As he did, a small stream of ashes poured to the ground. Mark gasped.

Emms just smiled. She tore the bag wide open, lifted it over her head, and twirled it with all her might. The ashes flew through the air. Some were caught by the wind and blew over the fence, some scattered around Mark and Emms. Mrs. MacKiver jumped back, but ashes sprinkled her as well.

"Ashes to ashes, dust to dust," Emms shouted triumphantly. "Now Rose will always be part of the library. The workmen will carry her ashes on their boots. She will be everywhere, including the garden that is going right here."

"I knew you were crazy, from the first time you came into the library." Connie MacKiver turned to Mark. "Listen kid, stay away from her."

She turned and stomped over to the security guard who had just arrived. He was carrying a cup of coffee. A friendly-looking dog was with him and it was eating a doughnut. Mark and Emms watched Connie as she yelled at the guard before leaving.

"I guess Rose won the last argument," Mark said.

"Nobody won any argument, but Rose got her wish," replied Emms. She looked at Mark and asked, "Am I a crazy old lady?"

Mark grinned. "That's why I like you."

Smiling, Emms picked up the empty jar and sat in the wheelchair. She said, "Tusen takk—that's Norwegian for 'a thousand thanks.' Thanks from me and thanks from Rose."

When they were back in the apartment elevator, Emms announced, "I am going to donate a chair to the library, a storyteller's chair, and I will have a small plaque put on it that says, 'Rose Reader, she loved stories and children.'"

And that is exactly what Emms did.

Fly Away

Paul Yee

BRITISH Columbia's gold lay buried in its vast, forbidding north, far from southern ports. Miners panned doggedly for nuggets in icy rivers, and tapped at mountains with feeble hammers. In the rugged bush, lonely towns supplied food and goods, barbers and entertainment. When winds whipped through the mountains, ramshackle wooden cabins whimpered and rattled as if earthquakes had hit.

In one such town, Old Joe ran the only Chinese store. He sold rice mixed with sand, marked at rooftop prices. On shelves stood earthenware jars of soured, moldy sauces set at the same high prices. The salt fish in his bins were hard as rock, yet Chinese miners still arrived to pick at them, for no other store sold food from their homeland.

Next door was Young Chan's tiny shack. Miners

who could neither read nor write came here to pay for letters to be written and read. Their families and loved ones lived far away and awaited New World news. Even Old Joe came because he had never attended school and knew only numbers and the names of his stock. He couldn't compose a sentence even if he stayed up all night.

One day, Old Joe ran into Young Chan's shop, waving a letter from China. "Quick!" he shouted. "Read this to me."

When unfolded, the rice paper revealed the most beautiful handwriting Young Chan had ever seen: "Honorable Sir, I have heard you are seeking a wife for the New World. My name is Mei-ping, I am an orphan of marrying age. I live in an abandoned temple and have nowhere to go. I will be your wife if you will have me. Send me a letter, tell me about yourself."

Old Joe jumped with glee. Young Chan thought he would crash through the floorboards. "At last I will have a wife," Old Joe crowed. "I thought no woman would come to this wilderness."

Young Chan did not hear. He gazed longingly at Mei-ping's words. How elegant they were, how perfect each brush stroke. The letter was a master-piece of art, a painting in black and white. *Only an exceptionally beautiful woman could compose this*, he told himself.

"Write quickly for me," Old Joe cried. "Tell her who I am, tell her what I own."

Young Chan picked up his brush and started a letter.

"Say that I am strong and healthy," ordered Old Joe, "a vigorous man of thirty."

"But—"

"Tell her I own a brick building with windows of sparkling colored glass."

"But—"

"Tell her my house is filled with books and paintings, servants and guards."

Young Chan protested, but to no avail. He wrote exactly as his customer instructed, even though every line told a lie. Old Joe was short and limped, lived alone behind a curtain in his storefront, and owned no books except for a ledger.

Weeks later, the old man ran in again. "Another letter came from Mei-ping," he shouted. "Read it quickly!"

"Honorable Sir," she wrote, "you have answered my prayers. A roof overhead and windows in the walls will let me read all day long. Books alone have brightened and warmed my cold lonely world. In return, I will make your heart full and content too."

Old Joe sighed dreamily. "Oh, she is perfect."

Young Chan sighed dreamily too. As he gazed at Mei-ping's letter, the grace of her brush strokes cast a love spell over him.

"Write another letter," ordered Old Joe. "Send her a ticket, some money, and the entry papers she needs. I shall marry her as soon as she arrives, before any more gray hair appears."

Young Chan groaned. How could such a cultured woman marry this old toad of a shopkeeper? He threw down his brush. When lies turned dangerous, Young Chan worried and grew fearful. An innocent young woman might get badly hurt this time. But if he didn't write the letter, he would lose a good customer and less food would appear on his table. Reluctantly, he wet his inkstone.

One dark night, several months later, a stage-coach clattered up to the store. Old Joe and Young Chan hurried forth and out stepped Mei-ping. Even by the bobbing light of their lanterns, they saw a woman more breathtaking than the words she had written. Her long hair glowed like lacquer, her cheeks were the color of ripening peaches, and her lips reminded the men of tiny red butterflies.

She bowed before Young Chan and spoke in a

voice as clear as a bell. "Honorable Sir, greetings. I am Mei-ping."

The letter writer blushed and stammered, "Y-you are mistaken." He pointed to Old Joe. "That is the man who will become your husband."

Mei-ping's eyes widened in shock at the sight of scraggly white whiskers and dry wrinkled skin. She realized all the letters had been lies. But Old Joe's gift money and ticket had already been used, so she quickly bowed to him and mumbled, "How grand a building you have. You look like a good man. I am happy to be here."

The wedding was the most colorful and the noisiest of celebrations ever to erupt in the mountains. In the days that followed, the townspeople watched Mei-ping pump water and hang up the wash. She always waved back politely. The store became filled with new aromas of fresh-steamed bread and the tang of spicy dishes. As Old Joe's appetite and waistline increased, so did his sense of kindness and fairness. He imported better grades of rice and fresher groceries to sell, all at reasonable prices. With needle and thread, Mei-ping mended the miners' clothes, so men always greeted her fondly. As the business prospered, Old Joe's heart swelled with love for his new bride.

One day, Mei-ping entered Young Chan's store and sat down wearily. Her face had lost its color and her eyes were dark with fatigue. "My life is not easy," she told Young Chan, "but I do not mind because this is the New World. They say change is never easy."

Young Chan fell to his knees. "Forgive me!" he cried out. "It was I who wrote those false words that brought you here."

Mei-ping sighed and made him stand up. "Do not pain yourself. These days, I no longer cry out from hunger or cold. I only wish you had not lied about the books. If I had known about that, I might never have come."

Young Chan hung his head in shame and held out his few books. "You are welcome to borrow these."

Mei-ping accepted them with a gracious nod and smiled for the first time in a long time.

When she returned them months later, winter had fallen and snow lay everywhere. Her complexion had regained its rosy cheer. "Thank you," she said. "Do you have any more books?"

Young Chan searched under his bed and through his trunk, but found nothing.

"I will read these ones again," Mei-ping declared.

"They are excellent books. I will enjoy them even more the second time."

When she returned them months later, winter was still with them. "Are you sure you don't have any other books?" she asked.

Young Chan shook his head. "I asked all my customers, but no one had books."

Mei-ping's eyes glistened with a hint of tears. "We live too far from the city, do we not?"

Young Chan declared, "We should all move there!"

She shook her head. "No, but more books should be delivered to us through the mountains. I often dream that the snowflakes falling around us are words twirling down from the sky. When they land on the ground, they slide onto pages and turn into books that the Goddess of the White Moon has sent me. You may think I'm silly, but books let my mind fly and soar. I will have to look for new ways to travel."

After she left, Young Chan cursed himself for deceiving her.

Early next morning there was a loud banging at his door. Old Joe stood there, pale and disheveled. "She's gone!" he called out weakly. "She took my horse and rode off. We must find her before the winter swallows her."

Quickly they borrowed horses and followed her tracks out of town. The forests stood silent and still. Sometimes they lost the trail where fresh snow had fallen. Sometimes fallen trees blocked their way. It became obvious that Mei-ping had gotten lost, for her tracks looped about in large circles, one way and then another, uphill and down. They rode for hours.

Soon night was falling, and falling swiftly. Old Joe moaned and shouted to the darkening sky, "Oh Heaven, please let her be alive. I love that woman more than my own life."

Finally the tracks took them high to the edge of a cliff. The hoof marks went only in one direction. The men dismounted and crawled forward careful-ly. They peeked over, raised their lanterns, and saw an enormous darkness yawning below. The wind howled around them like hungry wolves. Old Joe started weeping.

Young Chan suddenly pulled at him. "Look!"

Old Joe raised his head and looked at the moon, which had risen full and round. Far away on its shimmering surface, Mei-ping's face was smiling sadly. The two men gasped to see her familiar beauty glowing in the dark like a powerful lamp. Young Chan's lips were blue with cold when he whispered, "She has flown away to where the human imagination has longed to go."

The two men gazed skyward for a long time. Then they helped each other up, knowing they would never see Mei-ping again.

The entire town and all the store's customers wore black and mourned her for many months. And to this day, the families and descendants of the miners and shopkeepers of that town always think of Mei-ping when the full moon rises.

Books Don't Cry

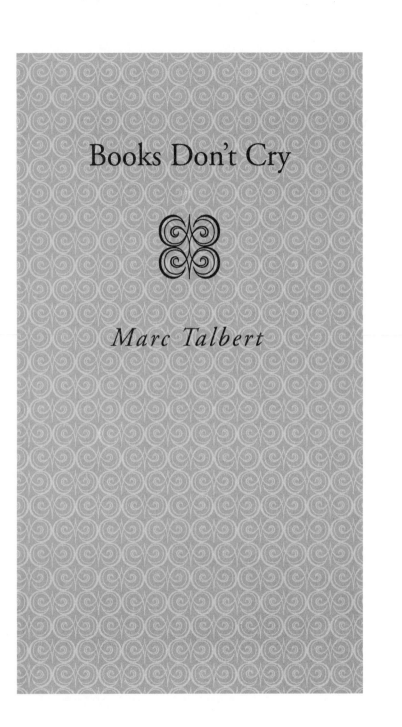

Marc Talbert

QUIETLY as he could, Tad Morgan climbed the creaking iron staircase that spiraled like a corkscrew from behind the main library desk on the first floor. Nobody had ever told him he couldn't go up here, but it felt forbidden. It was the adult section. Fiction. As his head popped above the second floor, his eyes opened wide. He felt almost giddy.

What he saw up here was better than anything he'd imagined.

Adult fiction felt like a place where he could flip to the next page if he didn't like what was happening—if he felt scared or felt like crying.

Tad stretched to look taller than twelve as he walked to the first aisle and peered down the rows of shelves. He liked the way the adult books looked, standing shoulder to shoulder.

It was such a relief to see that adult books were completely unlike children's books. Lately, kids' books had been driving Tad crazy. They came in too many sizes and thicknesses and colors—even the novels. And most of them had stains on them from food or sneezing. It embarrassed him to see kids' books shoved into their shelves with the edges of their pages exposed, white as underwear. And it irritated him that so many kids' books had puckered pages from rain or sweaty, sticky hands. Or from tears.

But here, in the adult section, the books were civilized. Soothing. Their colors were quiet. Some books were taller than others, and some were fatter. But he didn't see many that called attention to themselves. Silent and solid, they faced out, protecting each others' backsides.

He breathed deeply, still slightly winded from climbing the stairs and from being afraid someone would order him to come down. His nose crinkled at a faint tangy smell, as if the adult books were gently sweating. The smell reminded him of his grandmother and her room at the nursing home. Whether or not her clothes were newly washed, they never lost the smell of her on a hot July day, coming in from picking beans in the garden of her old house.

Tad felt comfortable in this adult-smelling section of the library. He liked to think he was pretty much grown-up. He wanted to be like these adult books, trim and unassuming on the outside, with a straight spine and square shoulders. Dignified.

He touched the gold lettering on a blue book. What would it be like to be a book? To be pulled from a shelf? To have someone flip through his pages, peering at his innermost thoughts?

He suddenly longed for someone to lift him from a shelf, to open him up. He imagined that person's eyes growing large. He imagined their heart beating faster at the march and swirl of the action, the razor wit and nimble intelligence of the hero that lived inside him.

He imagined that person coming to the end of him, reluctantly closing him up, tucking his story into covers—covers as tight and smooth as the ones on the hospital bed his grandmother now slept in.

He didn't want to think about his grandmother's bed.

Instead, Tad pulled his fingers from the blue book's gold lettering. He squared his shoulders and continued down the aisle. No book was out of line. He wouldn't be out of line, either, if he were a book. An adult book.

Tad frowned. As much as he liked the idea of being a book, there was only one trouble with it: books don't have heads.

He walked along, trying to imagine what a book's head would look like, if it had one. He couldn't. A book was too perfect the way it was. It was ridiculous to imagine a book with a head sticking up from its spine, bobbing about on a neck. It wouldn't make any difference what kind of head it was—old and kind and wise, or young and mischievous and clever—any kind of head would just get in a book's way. In Tad's way.

Tad often felt the same way about his own head. Perhaps, like a book, his life would be simpler, less complicated without one.

Almost shyly, Tad felt his own head, above his ears. He let his fingers sink beneath his hair. What he felt was apple shaped, which made sense. His head sometimes blushed, glowing red through the blond hair above his forehead. Once, glancing in the rearview mirror of his family's car, he'd seen it glow apple green when he was carsick.

Granny Smith. Delicious. From the state of Washington or from New Zealand. Whatever. His head might as well be an apple. How else could he explain the feel of wormy ideas squirming inside his head, eating crisscrossing tunnels through it? How else could he explain the feel of ideas twisting and turning, struggling for ways to escape?

Perhaps the lines of letters in books were just worms pulled from somebody's head and then stretched across paper, left to dry until each segment of each worm crumbled into a letter shape, the letter shapes clumping into words.

Now that he thought of it, pictures of the brain looked like balls of worms. Stretched out, how many thousands of lines of words could come from the brain of a writer?

It was a wonderfully disgusting thought and Tad smiled. He had always dreamed of being a writer. He loved reading and he loved inventing words, describing things. He was always making up stories in his head—what some old person had been like as a child, what some kid was going to be when he grew up. When Tad saw somebody hobbling around on a cast, pictures in his head told him how the leg had been broken. It wasn't always easy making up stories, but it was fun.

Yes, he'd always wanted to be a writer. An author, really, because "author" sounded so much more accomplished than "writer."

The only person Tad had ever told this to was his

grandmother. The last time he and his mother had visited the nursing home, his mother had gone off to complain about something in his grandmother's room. Tad had taken that opportunity to tell his grandmother that he wanted to write a famous novel someday. The trouble was, he confessed, he didn't know what he could write about that other people might want to read. His grandmother had smiled and told him that he'd surely write a novel someday and that she wanted the first copy, with his autograph inside.

He'd have to hurry to write it in time for his grandmother. But he didn't want to think about that.

Tad reached the end of the aisle and started down the next one, grateful to be calmed once more by the sameness of the adult books. His eyes bounced right and left, glancing off titles and the names of authors.

He realized what he had seen when he'd gone two steps past it. A medium-sized book, powder blue, looking new, with "Morgan" stamped on the spine.

Tad turned around and took two steps.

The book stood level with his eyes. There was no first name. But his last name fit perfectly. Tad let himself imagine that he was looking at a book he'd written. His smile floated toward his nose.

Why not? Why couldn't this book be his?

He looked at the books on either side. They looked like good company. He liked the idea of his book being among them.

Tad hooked a finger onto the book's collar, below the place where the book's head would have been, if books had heads. He tipped it, letting it fall into his other hand.

The title was strange: *Hot Cross Buns*. He was disappointed that it sounded like the title of a children's book. But he was pleased to see that the author's name was Ted Morgan. That first name could be altered very easily.

Wouldn't his grandmother be proud!

He crept down the spiral staircase, feeling more giddy than when he'd climbed up. The book felt hot in his palm.

It wasn't hard to slip the book into his backpack without checking it out. No alarms went off and no lights flashed blue and red.

At home, he rushed into his bedroom and closed the door. He flipped the book open to the title page. Using his pocketknife, he scraped off the *e* in "Ted." He was careful not to tear a hole in the paper. Even more carefully, he used his finest felt-tipped pen to replace the *e* with an *a*.

The book was his. Tad Morgan's.

Except for the dedication. Who was "Rosie, who smiles like an angel," anyway?

On a blank piece of paper, he typed: "For Grandmother Bacon, who reads me like a book." He coated the back of the paper with rubber cement and pressed it over the dedication page. He smoothed it out and then trimmed the edges to match. Tad eyed it critically. A person would have to be really picky to notice.

Piling pillows at the head of his bed, Tad flopped onto his back, eager to read. The book began with great promise: "One of the few places darker than Winthrop's brain was the inside of a hog's stomach." The next sentence was a bog of details, followed by a couple lines of stupid dialogue. Tad's eyes skidded to a stop when he got to the first bad word.

If he showed this book to his grandmother, that word would have to go. Tad glanced at the next couple of sentences. There were more bad words, all different. He grabbed his felt-tipped pen and carefully blotted them out. What else could he do?

It took until dinner to blot out the bad words in the first three chapters. It took the rest of the week to go through the remainder of the book. The print was tiny. There were three hundred and forty-six pages and seven hundred and sixty-three bad words.

The most interesting thing about the book was the sheer number of bad words. The story was pathetic beyond belief. Why would one man want so many girlfriends? And why would any woman want to fall in love with a man who didn't care about anybody except himself? Tad thought the book could use a few illustrations to perk it up, so he drew one for each chapter. He jammed them in the cracks between the pages, after he dribbled enough rubber cement there to make them stick.

There were whole pages of smooching and worse. Using his pocketknife, he cut out these unnecessary pages carefully, so that nobody would miss them unless they were sticklers for page numbers skipping.

He worked on the book for the next two weeks. Fixing the book was harder than he imagined writing a book would be in the first place. Was the finished book worth it? It read pretty well—once he got used to skipping over all the blackened blocks that used to be bad words, and the block shaped ghosts that had soaked through to the other side of the paper. His illustrations were great. And he'd typed out a new ending, replacing the last sixteen pages with four of his own. Winthrop now got what he deserved—and a certain hog wasn't going to need to eat again for a week.

It had been fun playing God.

Tad was nervous taking the book to his grandmother. It had become more than a book to him. He had put a lot of himself into the book. It felt like him, Tad Morgan, in book form. He was desperate for his grandmother to like it. To like him.

As soon as his mother left the room to complain about something, Tad took the book from his backpack and handed it to his grandmother. She looked puzzled as she opened it. He watched her flip through the first couple of pages and was relieved to see her smile when she looked up.

"The dedication," she said. "Thank you."

Footsteps came from the hallway and she slipped the book under a pillow just before Tad's mother came in, dragging an orderly behind her.

Back home, Tad grew nervous as he pictured his grandmother reading the book. Did she like it? Had he done a good enough job? Were the blackened words too distracting? Maybe he should have started from scratch and written something that was less work to read.

Two days before he and his mother were to visit his grandmother again, his mother stepped into his bedroom without knocking. She looked as if she'd been crying.

"Your grandmother is being taken to the hospital," she said. "Get a jacket. Now. Your father is coming home from work to drive us there."

His grandmother looked terrible. She had tubes in her nose and tubes in her wrists. Her hair was uncombed and flecks of blood scabbed her lips. Her smile was weak when she saw Tad.

His parents stayed by the door as he stepped up to her. She beckoned him to lean close. "My author."

He wanted to ask, "Did you like me?" Instead he asked, "Did you like the book?"

She shook her head.

He nodded, crushed.

"Tell your own stories," she whispered. "Your own stories will be much better." She fumbled for his hand. "Don't worry. Just take your time. You'll make a fine book."

Was she talking about the book he would write? Or the book—headless and dignified—that he sometimes longed to be? Or had she meant both of those things? He didn't know, but he nodded again and tried to smile as his grandmother's fingers slipped from his. Stepping aside, he made way for his parents.

Tad watched them bend over his grandmother. Her words echoed in his head: "You'll make a fine book." Whatever she had meant, Tad didn't feel anything like a book.

Books don't cry.

The Mystery of the Cuddly Wuddly Bunny

Tim Wynne-Jones

WHEN I was ten, I met a boy who wanted to be the first person to see the Pacific Ocean. I was in the library at the time—I was always in the library.

"Excuse me?" I said. I was sitting at a table with a book open in front of me. He was in the window seat, my favorite place. Except it's hard to sit there when you're reading a very large book.

"I'd like to be the first person to see the Pacific Ocean," he said.

"The Pacific's only seven blocks away," I said.

The boy made a face. "I mean the *first* person to see it."

I looked past the boy out the window. You couldn't see the ocean from here, just people passing by, traffic. There were some kids. I wondered if they were bullies waiting for him. Maybe he was trapped. He didn't look trapped. He didn't look frightened. Maybe he was nuts.

There was nothing else I could think of to say, so I returned my attention to *The Very Large Book of Explorers*. I had just finished a chapter on Columbus. I turned the page and there was a full-color painting of the Spanish conquistador, Vasco Núñez de Balboa. He was wearing his conquistador armor, carrying a sword in one hand and a banner in the other, and wading out into the ocean. I read the caption: "1513—Balboa discovers the Pacific Ocean and claims it for Spain."

I felt shivery inside. I glanced up at the mystery boy. He was looking out the window. Was it a coincidence? Of course not. He had obviously read the same book and was just trying to make conversation.

He twisted around to look at me.

"You're four hundred years too late," I said.

"For what?"

"For being the first person to see the Pacific Ocean."

The boy rolled his eyes. "You think Balboa was the first person to see the Pacific?" He shook his head, exasperated. "Those explorers," he said in a cranky voice as if he was talking about someone he knew; as if he was saying, "Those kids from Irwin Park," or something. "They head off somewhere and get native guides to lead them to a giant waterfall or a river or an ocean or whatever, and then they write home and say *they* discovered it."

It was something I had never thought about before. But it was true. In the painting there were natives. Probably guides.

"If Balboa was around right now," said the boy, "he'd probably walk in here and claim this library for Spain. Can you see it?"

I could. I could see Balboa barging through the doors, marching right up to Miss Staple, the librarian, and planting his flag on her ink pad.

"I claim this library for Spain!" he would shout. And Miss Staple would tell him, nicely, to lower his voice.

I laughed out loud. I looked over to the boy but he was gone. (Seeing things in your head sometimes takes a few minutes.) When I left, I asked Miss Staple if she had seen him before. "Who?" she asked.

"A kid. About my age."

She grinned, raised an eyebrow. "If you are seriously planning on becoming a writer, you'd better work on your powers of observation."

I took the long way home, down along the ocean front. It was the Pacific Ocean but it was just West Van. It wasn't like in the book. No big breakers rolling in. No palm trees. No conquistadors.

◌◌

I only ever saw the boy at the library. The second time, it was a rainy Saturday and I was curled up in the window seat with *Prisoners of the Xingu*. The fall rain was coming down hard, gusting against the glass. People outside were hurrying by, their faces hidden under umbrellas. But in the book it was steamy hot—the Amazon jungle. I finished a chapter and raced to the washroom. When I returned, the mystery boy was in my place reading my book.

"Listen to this," he said. "'The jungle river was swarming with piranhas.'"

I nodded, excitedly. "It's pretty good, huh?"

He wrinkled his nose. "I guess, but it's a bit obvious. Why not: 'the jungle river was swarming with ballerinas.'"

"What?"

He shrugged. "You've got to admit it would be more surprising."

I made a face.

"Hey," he said. "Ballerinas can be pretty frightening when they get kicking." My sister was a ballerina; I knew what he meant. I sat down; there was just enough room on the window seat for both of us. "Or," he said, "it could be swarming with spaghetti."

The laughter leaped out of my throat as big as a jaguar and just as unwelcome in a library.

"Well, you've got to admit it would be interesting," he said. I nodded, but I was already flipping back through the book.

"Listen to this one," I said. "'Alfonso hid behind the rock, his gun oiled and ready.'" I looked up at the mystery boy, expectantly.

"Hmmm," he said, his eyes flashing. "How about: 'Alfonso hid behind the rock, his lobster boiled and ready.'"

It became a game. We scoured *Prisoners of the Xingu* for obvious stuff—there was tons—and filled in the blanks with words of our own. "The air above the trading post buzzed with waffles." "He drew a slim silver case from his breast pocket, flipped it open, and took out a goldfish which he placed between his feet and lit with a silver refrigerator." "Get out of here, Bart, and may your shadow never darken my lemon meringue pie again."

I went to borrow a pencil from Miss Staple to

write some of this stuff down. When I got back—
you guessed it—he was gone.

Miss Staple was putting an atlas back in the reference section. I described the boy to her. She raised
her eyebrow.

"You might almost be describing yourself," she
said.

I was disappointed, but I took out *Prisoners of the
Xingu* and wrote pages of unobvious sentences,
hoping he might be at the library next time I was
there. He wasn't. Nor the next time. Finally, I
stopped expecting to see him. I almost forgot all
about him.

It was the following spring that I ran into him for
the third and last time. I didn't see him right away.
He wasn't in his usual place which was *my* usual
place. He was over in the Kiddies' Corner, sitting
on a bright blue cushion and leaning against the
wall with a picture book open in his lap.

"*The Cuddly Wuddly Bunny?*" I said.

He looked up and grinned.

"I was feeling a bit sad," he said, "so I've been
reading picture books."

There was a pile of them beside him. I recog-
nized some old favorites of my own from when I
was little.

"It's a good mystery," he said.

The Cuddly Wuddly Bunny a mystery? This was news to me.

I guess he saw the surprise on my face. "Read it," he said. So I curled up on a bright red cushion and started reading. It sure wasn't a mystery who drew the picture of the car on page five. That was me. I was trying to copy the Cuddly Wuddly Bunny's car, the one he drove all over the countryside looking for The Face He Knew Best In The Whole World. The car—my car—had been rubbed out as best as I could, but it was still there. And although I knew it wasn't a great idea to be drawing in library books, it was kind of nice to find a bit of myself in the book after so many years.

Maybe you haven't read *The Cuddly Wuddly Bunny*. Well, the Cuddly Wuddly Bunny isn't really a bunny but a full-grown rabbit. He has a family of his own but he feels lonely one bright fall day, so he goes off looking for The Face He Knows Best In The Whole World. He thinks maybe he's looking for his father. His dad has a pleasant, handsome face but it isn't the one Cuddly Wuddly seems to be looking for. Next he sees his mother. She sure has a lovely warm face but it isn't the face he remembers, either. He goes through all his old dolls and teddies, then his best school pal and his favorite teacher. As glad as he is to see them and they are to see him, none of them have the face he sees in his mind— The Face He Knows Best In The Whole World. At the end of a long day, he heads home to his wife and kids, thinking how good it will be to see their sparkly faces because he loves them very much. All his bunnies in their jammies greet him at the door with hugs and kisses. So the last page in the book is the house and you can see Cuddly Wuddly through the window reading to his kids who are all over him. But what you see most is the full moon shining down on his house. And the man in the moon is smiling most beautifully.

I didn't know what I liked about the book when I was a kid—probably the car—but I knew that what I liked most about it now was that the writer didn't explain at the end. He just left it up to me to figure out.

"You're right," I said. "It is a mystery." But when I looked up, my library friend was gone again.

☉☉

By then I was eleven and writing quite a lot, myself. Not just assignments for school, my own stories. And I always tried to write them as if I was discovering something for the very first time, no matter how many stories other people had written about the same subject. I tried never to be obvious. And I tried to remember that every story is a mystery even if there isn't a corpse in it and there isn't any lost pirate gold. The mystery is what makes you turn the pages, what makes you read to the end.

These are the three things I learned from my mysterious library friend. I never saw him again. And what's weird is that I never saw *The Cuddly Wuddly Bunny* again. The book disappeared from the library. At first I figured he had taken it. I figured that's why he didn't come around anymore.

Years passed. Recently, I found myself thinking about that book again. So I looked in my local library, in all the reference sources—all over the place—but I could not find *The Cuddly Wuddly Bunny*.

I mentioned this to Miss Staple when I was out west to visit my folks. She had retired by then, but we had become friends so I dropped around to her place for a visit. She didn't remember the book any more than she remembered the mystery boy.

She smiled at me, though, as she poured us each another Artichoke & Blueberry Fizz. "It would make a great idea for a story," she said.

Contributors

Sarah Ellis has worked as a children's librarian and taught children's literature at colleges and universities in North America, Europe, and Japan. For over a decade, she was a regular columnist for *The Horn Book Magazine.* Sarah is the author of several highly-praised books for young people, including *Pick-Up Sticks,* which won a Governor General's Literary Award. Her recent work includes *The Young Writer's Companion.* Sarah lives in Vancouver, British Columbia.

Michele Landsberg still loves children's books, and is a member of CBC Radio's children's book panel—a good excuse to keep reading them. Her critical guide to children's literature was published in Canada as *Michele Landsberg's Guide to Children's Books,* in the U.S. as *Reading for the Love of It,* and in the U.K. as *The World of Children's Books.* It was recommended by *The London Times* as a gift book for the royal family and was on best-seller lists in Canada and England. Michele lives in Toronto, Ontario.

Jean Little's stories are loved by children everywhere; her books have been translated into French, German, Greek,

Danish, Dutch, Norwegian, and Japanese, among other languages. Her large, award-winning body of work includes short stories and poems, as well as picture books and novels. A Member of the Order of Canada, Jean lives in Guelph, Ontario, on the same street as the library.

Celia Barker Lottridge started out as a children's librarian in the U.S. These days, she is a Toronto-based storyteller; she has also helped develop the Parent-Child Mother Goose Program, a community service in which nursery rhymes and stories are used with children and their parents. Celia is the author of several highly-successful picture books, including *Music for the Tsar of the Sea*, and three delightful novels: *Ticket to Curlew*, *The Wind Wagon*, and *Wings to Fly*.

Ken Roberts is chief librarian of the Hamilton Public Library, as well as a storyteller, puppeteer, magician, and juggler. He is the author of several humorous novels for children including *Hiccup Champion of the World*, *Pop Bottles*, *Past Tense*, *Crazy Ideas*, and *The Thumb in the Box*. Ken lives near Brantford, Ontario, with his wife and their two children.

Ken Setterington is very familiar with libraries. He is Children and Youth Advocate for Library Services for the Toronto Public Library and teaches in the Faculty of Information Studies at the University of Toronto. He is a well-known book reviewer and storyteller. His first book, a retelling of Hans Christian Andersen's *The Snow Queen*, was published in 2000. "Rose's Wish" is based on Ken's experience helping a friend scatter ashes under a library. Ken lives in Toronto, Ontario.

Marc Talbert has published thirteen novels, several of which have been translated into such languages as Spanish, Danish, Norwegian, German, French, and Japanese. His latest books include *Small Change*, *The Trap*, *Star of Luís*, *Heart of a Jaguar*, and *A Sunburned Prayer*. Marc lives in Tesuque, New Mexico, with his wife and their two daughters.

Budge Wilson was born and educated in Nova Scotia, where she lives in a fishing village. She worked for many years as a fitness instructor and was also a teacher and photographer. Although she began writing later in life, Budge has since published more than twenty books, with editions in ten countries and eight languages. In 1994, her award-winning work won a coveted place on the American Library Association list, "The 75 Best (Children's) Books of the Last 25 Years."

Tim Wynne-Jones is the multi-talented author of books for all audiences. His series of books about Zoom, an enigmatic cat, has brought him wide acclaim. Tim's work has received many honors, including the prestigious Boston Globe-Horn Book Award, and he is a two-time winner of the Governor General's Literary Award. His most recent book is *The Boy in the Burning House*. Tim lives with his family in eastern Ontario.

Paul Yee, whose family came to Canada in the first wave of Chinese migration at the turn of the century, grew up in Vancouver's Chinatown. He has published numerous children's books on the experiences of the Chinese in Canada, including *Tales From Gold Mountain*, *Roses Sing on New*

Snow, and *Ghost Train*, which won a Governor General's Literary Award. A former archivist, Paul now lives in Toronto where he writes full-time.